42
Indian Mandalas
COLORING BOOK

Monika Helwig

*with an Introduction
by Wolfgang Hund*

Hunter House PUBLISHERS
Alameda, CA

Ordering

Trade bookstores in the U.S. and Canada please contact:

    Publishers Group West
    1700 Fourth Street, Berkeley CA 94710
    Phone: (800) 788-3123   Fax: (510) 528-3444

Hunter House books are available at bulk discounts for textbook course adoptions; to qualifying community, health care, and government organizations; and for special promotions and fund-raising. For details please contact:

    Special Sales Department
    Hunter House Inc., PO Box 2914, Alameda CA 94501-0914
    Phone: (510) 865-5282   Fax: (510) 865-4295
    E-mail: ordering@hunterhouse.com

Individuals can order our books from most bookstores, by calling toll-free (800) 266-5592, or from our website at **www.hunterhouse.com**

Project Credits

Illustrations: Monika Helwig	Cover Design & Book Production: Jil Weil
Translator: André Kuehnemund	Copy Editors: Kiran Rana, Alexandra Mummery
Acquisitions Editor: Jeanne Brondino	Associate Editor: Alexandra Mummery
Editorial & Production Assistant: Emily Tryer	Acquisitions & Publicity Assistant: Lori Covington
Publicity Manager: Sara Long	Sales & Marketing Assistant: Earlita K. Chenault
Customer Service Manager: Christina Sverdrup	Order Fulfillment: Joel Irons
Administrator: Theresa Nelson	Computer Support: Peter Eichelberger
Publisher: Kiran S. Rana	

Printed and bound by Bang Printing, Brainerd, Minnesota

Manufactured in the United States of America

9 8 7 6 5 4 3 2   First Edition   03 04 05

An Introductory Note...

Mandalas, like the ones in this coloring book, have been used for relaxation, meditation, and recreation for centuries by people in many different cultures. In the following text we have suggested how mandalas can be used in the classroom by teachers and educators, but mandalas are for everyone to use and enjoy. We hope you will feel free to try out our suggestions at home, at work, or wherever you choose, and modify them creatively to suit your needs.

Mandalas...the Cool, New Thing?

Those who have been teachers for any length of time have probably experienced how quickly the excitement over an innovative new method of instruction subsides. The techniques that survive are always the well-established ones that have proven successful in most situations in daily school life—and that suit differing individual teaching styles.

Mandalas have been trendy in Europe for quite some time—celebrated in New Age circles as a method for finding oneself and recommended as a therapeutic defense against stress and psychosomatic problems. The many books and articles written about them have led to these circle-motifs often being equated with esotericism and New Age psychology.

However, the fact of the matter is that mandalas are much older and more cross-cultural than the New Age movement. The round, stained-glass windows in gothic cathedrals prove that the soothing, reflective, and peaceful effect of this kind of composition has long been recognized in the Western world. The circle is a basic form both in nature and in culture. It automatically draws attention to its center and has therefore served as a thought-collecting and reflective aid since prehistoric times. It is this quality that can be used in the classroom to help children find both peace and quiet.

Teaching Peace and Quiet

Quiet is a basic requirement for all children, a fact that Maria Montessori and others have emphasized.

By quiet I do not mean an external, forced absence of sound brought about by strict discipline. This only results in tension, conflicts, and restlessness. Rather I mean an inner peace in which the children can retreat into themselves, collect their thoughts, concentrate, and reflect; an inner composure that can only flourish in the appropriate atmosphere. It is the teacher's task to both create and retain this atmosphere, and to achieve this the teacher must be prepared to try something new. Using these mandalas in the classroom can create this type of quiet space for children.

Different Ways of Using Mandalas

There are three main ways to use mandalas:

- looking at them
- coloring them in
- creating your own

The first two options can be carried out easily with a minimum of teacher preparation. I believe there should be no set ways for or rules about using mandalas in class, so the following suggestions are intentionally brief.

Looking at Mandalas

- Project a colored mandala (e.g., a gothic stained-glass window) using a slide projector or an overhead projector (a colored-in overhead transparency).
- Look at the mandala as a group, either in silence or with suitable, relatively quiet background music.
- After several minutes of reflection, talk about the mandala (though this is not necessary).
- After showing the children a colored overhead, project a blank copy of the mandala and ask the children to think of their own colors. After about 3 minutes, give them a copy of the mandala to color in.

Coloring-in Mandalas

- It would go against the aim of the exercise for children to have to color in a mandala that they don't like. For this reason, there should always be a selection from which they can choose.
- Make sure that the situation is suitable (that there is enough time, sufficient lighting, a sign on the classroom door...).
- Photocopy the mandalas onto white, 8.5" x 11"-sized paper (or larger, if possible).

- Different ways of doing the coloring are possible, experiment with them:
  — coloring individually;
  — coloring in pairs (enlarge the mandala onto larger paper); the children can work at the same time or take turns;
  — coloring in a group (enlarge the mandala onto even larger paper); not more than four children per group.
- Give various time limits:
  — have children work on their mandalas until everyone is finished (provide extra tasks for those who finish first);
  — give the children a certain time limit (at least 20 minutes), and have them finish their mandalas during free time;
  — have the coloring time spread out over the week (for complicated mandalas), color in one section every day in free time, before the lesson begins, or between lessons.
- A box of mandalas placed in the free-play area can provide children with an interesting new opportunity. This idea can be used at home, too (often the enthusiasm is passed onto the parents, who in turn learn to relax together with their children—not the worst thing that a school can achieve!).
- For a parents' evening—consider trying mandalas as a change of pace!
- While coloring in
  — there is silence and no talking (not even in pair or group work) and/or
  — there is music playing quietly in the background (classical music, meditative music, etc.).
- Not every part of the mandala has to be colored in; some parts can be left white intentionally.
- Provide art supplies for the children to use for coloring in the mandalas—as many different colors as possible:
  — felt pens/markers (bright/fluorescent colors)
  — colored pencils
  — water colors and crayons (for bigger mandalas)
  — a mixture of the above
- Choose the colors consciously (contrasting colors, color families or palettes, warm and/or cold colors, by feel) or by chance (with closed eyes).
- Pass the mandala on to another child after a certain period of time; after a while, hand it back or pass it on to other children—this provides the children with experience in sharing and cooperation.
- Usually mandalas are colored from the inside out, but the children should feel free to do as they please. There is no "right" or "wrong" way to color in a mandala!

- When the children have finished, they can hang their mandalas on the board or around the room. This creates a fascinating combination of pictures. To wrap up the event, look at all of the pictures as a group (in silence or with background music) and finally discuss them ("I like this one because…").
- The finished mandalas make a colorful wall decoration that will invite the viewer to absorb, relax, and even talk about it.

Creating Your Own Mandalas

This is often the hardest part, because some children find it especially hard to draw on a blank piece of paper. Particularly in classrooms that have fairly strict settings, students often fear that they might do something "wrong" if they give into their moods and give free reign to their imaginations. Sadly, this inhibition is something that our children actually learn, and this learning process frequently happens for the very first time when they are in school.

Just as the mandala patterns in this book aren't perfect (they were handmade, using rulers and other tools, etc.), we shouldn't expect children to be able to draw a perfect, beautiful mandala. A first step could be providing half of a mandala to a child or at least a circle with a center point.

Whether one wants to or should first draw the outlines with a pencil, whether one should use rulers, masks, etc., or simply start drawing freehand using color pencils should be totally up to each individual. At the same time, you (as a teacher) should be able to draw a mandala relatively easily, and thereby encourage the children.

Something you might want to do (not at the very beginning, but after having done this for a little while) is to design mandalas that have a theme. This can be done with a partner or in groups, using themes like:

- Christmas/Easter/Halloween/the seasons
- Mother's Day/vacations
- plants/nature/flowers/trees
- triangles/squares/circles/spirals
- …

If someone gets "stuck" while designing a mandala, it is sometimes a good plan to simply put it aside for a while and try again later. Often, the flow of ideas will suddenly reappear if you take a break.

So, to end this Introduction: Try it for yourself!
You will see that school can be fun—for students and teachers!

Wolfgang Hund
Hersbruck, Germany

More About Indian Mandalas

A mandala is a drawing, usually in the form of a circle or polygon, that is often used as a tool for reflection and centering. Over time, the use of certain symbols in the drawings can also help in developing visualization skills.

In the West, the use of mandalas as a tool for relaxation is still often considered a novelty and is often limited to coloring books. However, the fact that both "small" as well as "large" human beings can relax by coloring mandalas proves that they can serve as a meditation aid in our hemisphere as well. Getting absorbed in coloring mandalas helps us to unplug, to focus our thoughts on ourselves, and to focus on what's important.

The enclosed collection primarily contains *kolam* patterns that are still used in India today. They contain a wide range of symbols and designs that have been passed on through many generations.

A Little History

Religious or sacred mandalas in India seem to have their origin in Buddhism, where they were used as a visual aid for meditation. The original diagrams followed strictly regulated forms that reflected the world as it was seen by Buddhism. These mandalas were supposed to call upon demons, ghosts, and even gods to serve the people who created them.

Traditional Buddhist mandalas contained symbols that were connected with specific deities. These symbols were arranged in a geometric form and could be made on a number of different levels, from highly abstract to very detailed. The colors used in these mandalas also followed special rules. The most common rules were that yellow symbolized earth (soil), red stood for fire, white for water, green for air, and blue for ether—"heaven's scent."

If we think about the phrase "coming full circle" for a moment, we realize that a circle also directs attention to its center. In meditation, the center or focus is the inner self, the center, so in a mandala the center is usually an important figure in Buddhist religion, a teacher or a god.

The meditative ritual is to look at the mandala analytically for a while, then "dive" into its center, visualizing the deity in the center until it becomes the real Buddha in one's mind. By utilizing special hand gestures *(Mudras)* and prayer spells *(Mantras)*, the practitioner becomes able to stay focused on the Buddha-figure and become one with it.

Mandala Symbolism

Most likely, not all forms and symbols in this book have a deeper meaning. However, several themes appear over and over again and should be interpreted as symbolic.

Most kolams show flowers in various forms. In Buddhism, there are three different kinds of flowers that have deeper meanings. The most important of them is the fully bloomed lotus, symbolic of the rise from the ancient ocean, free from any sins of the world.

Another frequently used element is a flaming jewel, which serves as a symbol of enlightenment.

Peacock feathers are a symbol of the redemption of sins, which is why we often find peacock imagery in mandalas.

Entire mandalas or parts of mandalas that seem to consist of continuous lines with no beginning or end are symbols of the never-ending twists and turns in life. A broken line means that there will be ups and downs in life and many expectations will remain unfulfilled.

The seashell, often simplified as a spiral, symbolizes teaching and learning and is also a symbol of listening.

Mandalas Today

Even though mandalas still contain a variety of Buddhist symbols, many have been "simplified" into decorative collections of geometric forms. However, mandalas serve ritual and meditative purposes even today. Usually, the meditative ritual today begins with the making of the mandala. As a result, almost every one has its own little history.

Frequently, Indian kolams are "painted" on the ground using rice flour, rice paste, dyed sand, stones, flowers, leaves, and many other things. They are also frequently painted at dawn in front of the entrances to homes. The reasons and occasions vary. They may be created to keep evil spirits away, to relieve someone's suffering, or to invite fertility. During celebrations, the entire house may be decorated with kolams.

In Indian elementary schools, children may draw kolams on the ground using rice flour. The children are usually immersed in what they are doing and seem to enjoy what their hands are capable of creating. Because the drawings are often 3 ft. or more in diameter, the children are in constant motion. The capability to turn an image in their minds into something visible enhances concentration, creativity, and their ability to learn.

In the West, mandala patterns are being used today as a way to relax and focus or as a way to unleash one's creative side. If you are a teacher, it doesn't matter whether you try them out yourself or not or what the purpose is behind using them—the important thing is to let your students choose the ones they like and can enjoy. Some children will fill in the patterns with bright colors. Others will choose darker colors, while some may enhance the patterns with their own symbols.

Ideas for the Classroom

If using mandalas in class gets you positive feedback from your students, try to discuss the subject with them. You could try to awaken an interest in the origin and purpose of a mandala and, by doing so, open a connection to the culture that inspired them. Tell your students about their origin and symbols and how Indian women use mandalas today. Your students may want to create their own mandala patterns. You may want to create some as well! By sharing your own experiences, you will encourage your students to be creative. And remember, the results don't have to be perfect pieces of art. This is simply an exercise designed to help us relax. The result is not just what is drawn, but also the feelings that arise inside us while we are working on the mandalas.

Finally, I would like to encourage you to try out the "Indian" version of this activity sometime. On a beautiful day, take your students outside and let them paint mandalas in the schoolyard. The best tools for these decorative purposes are, of course, chalk, flowers, tree leaves, stones, and tree fruits (during the fall). You'll see how relaxing and inspiring this creative and meditative alternative is—all done while breathing fresh air.

No matter how you end up using the kolams, I hope you'll have lots of fun with them!

Monika Helwig
Essen, Germany

The Mandalas

1   2   3   4   5   6

7   8   9   10   11   12

13   14   15   16   17   18

19   20   21   22   23   24

25   26   27   28   29   30

31   32   33   34   35   36

37   38   39   40   41   42

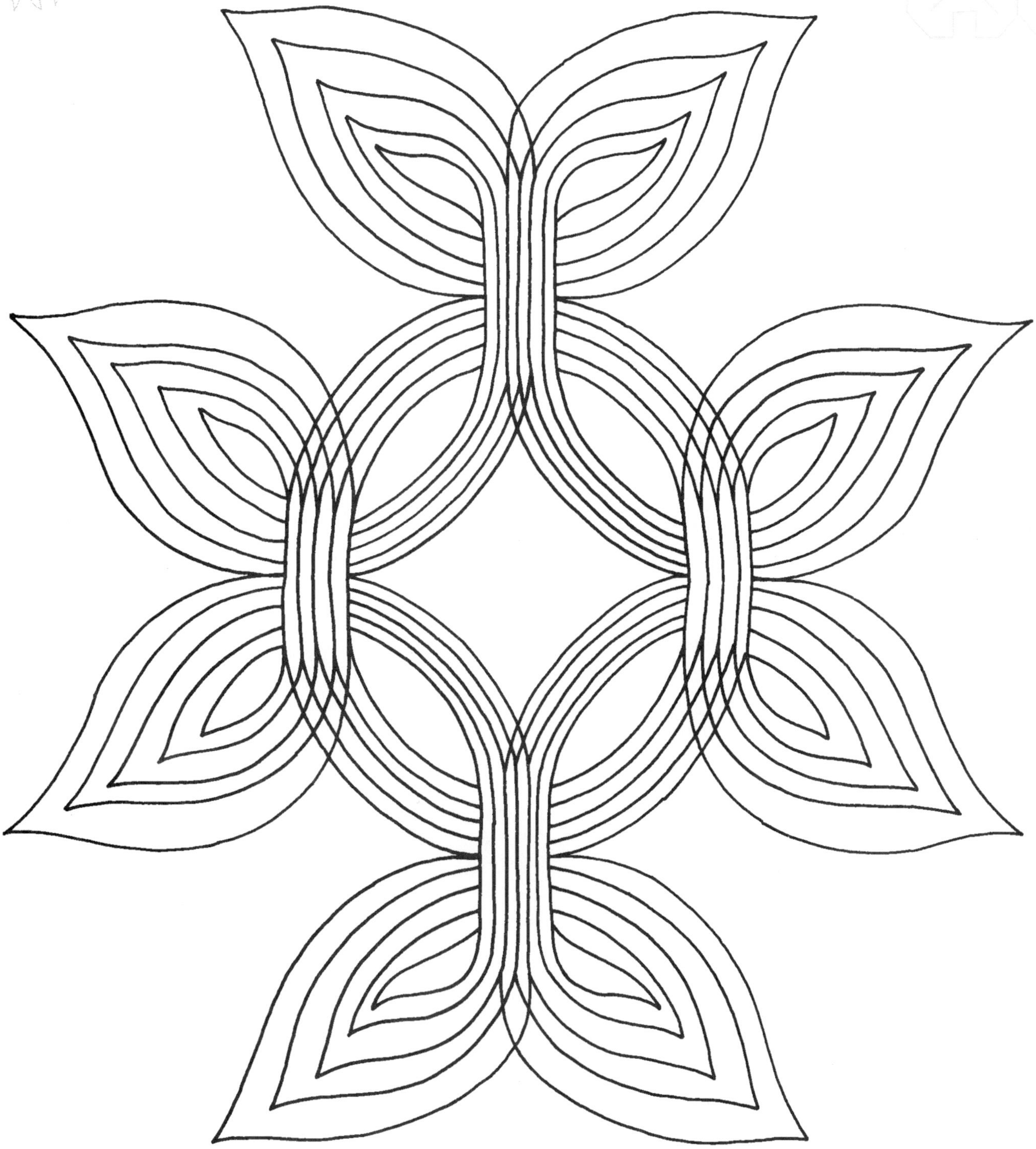

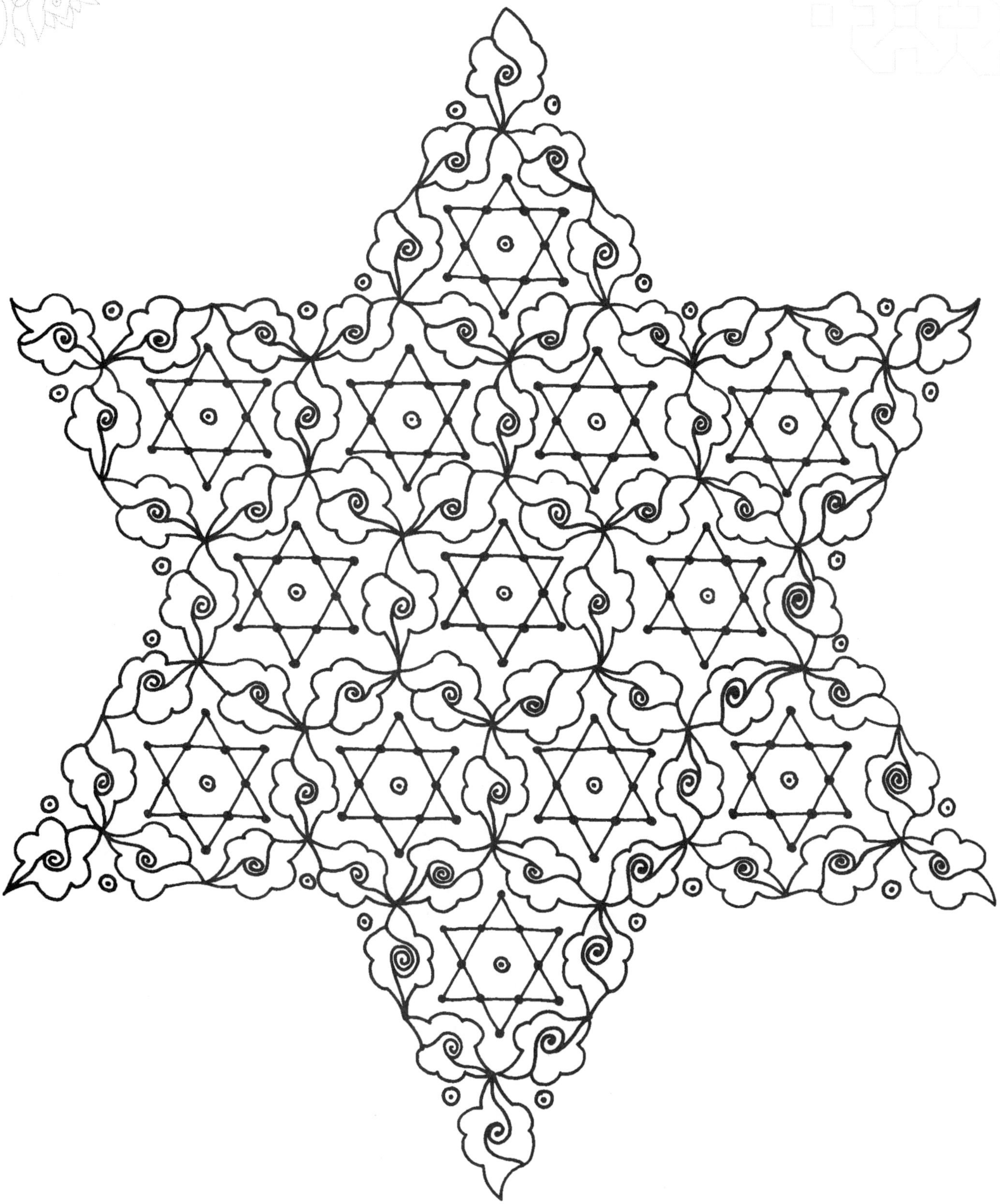

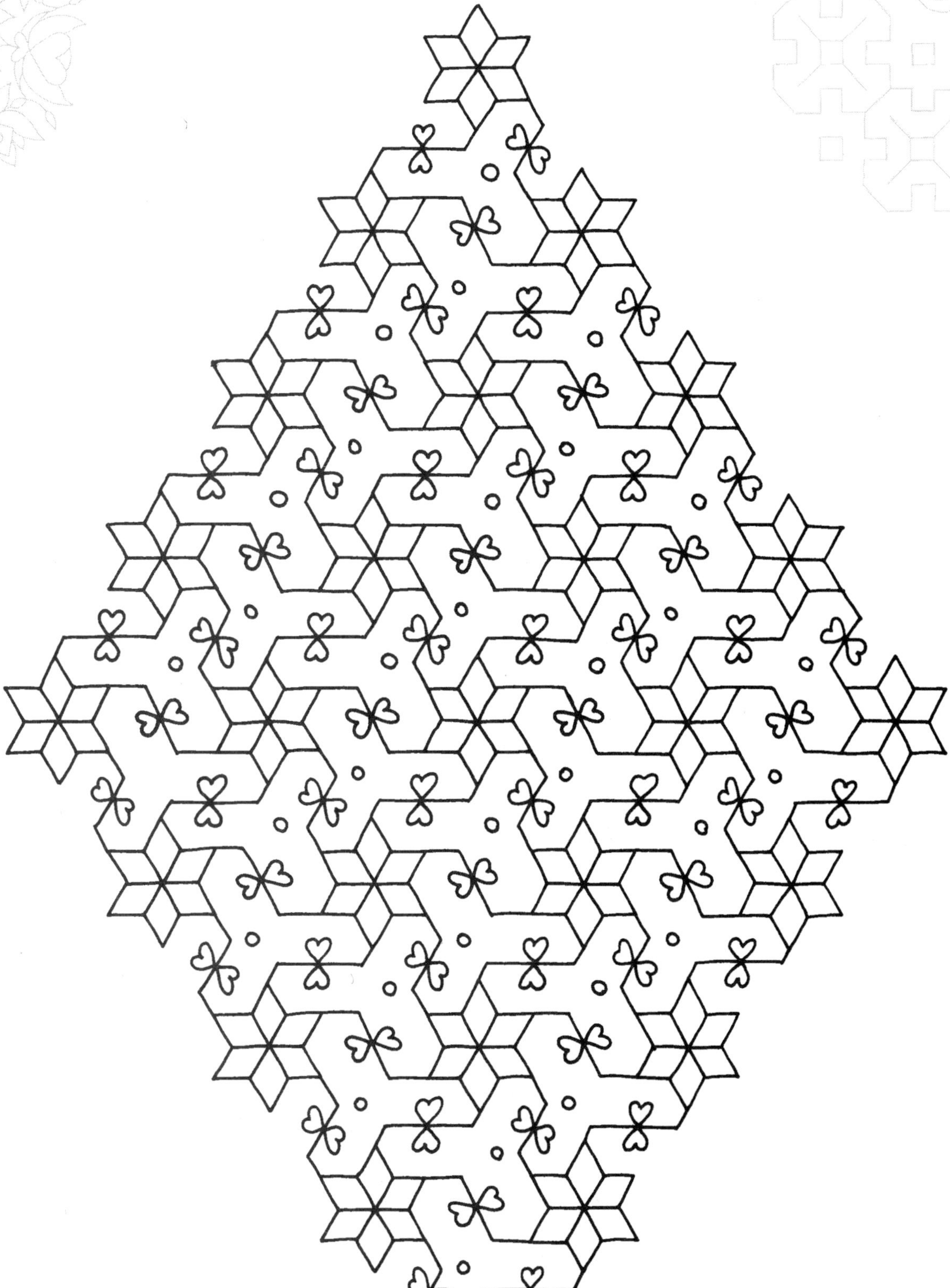

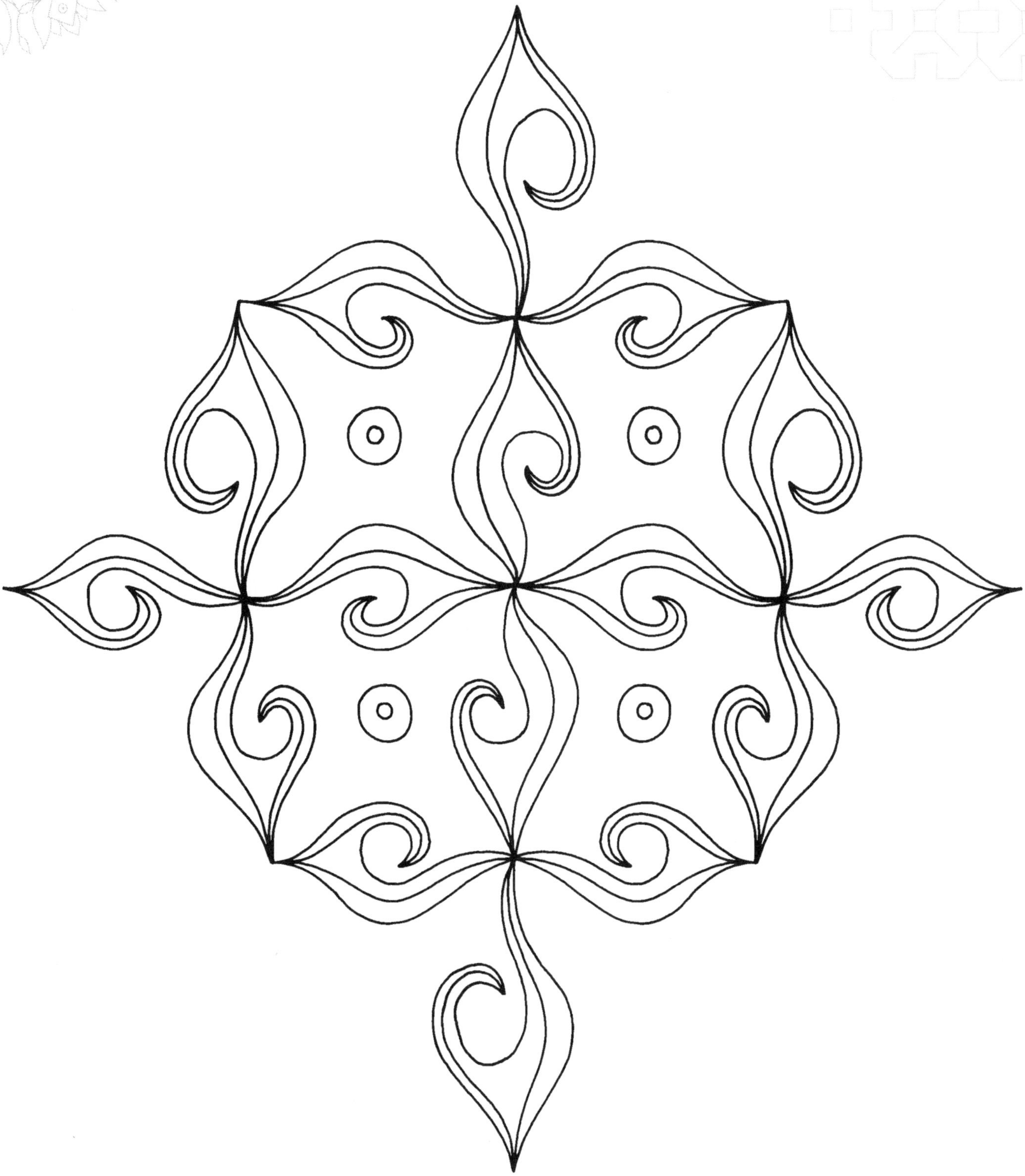

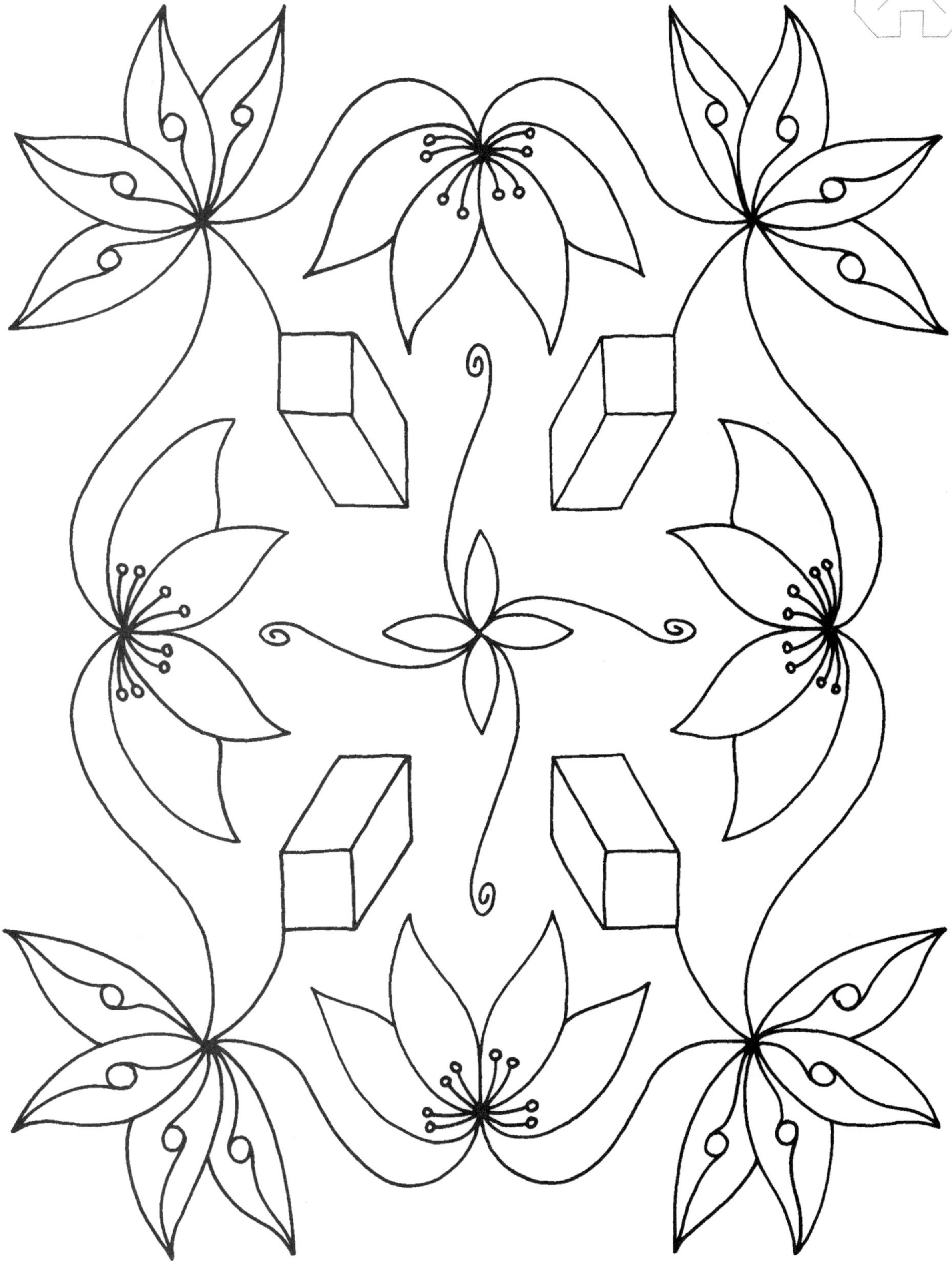

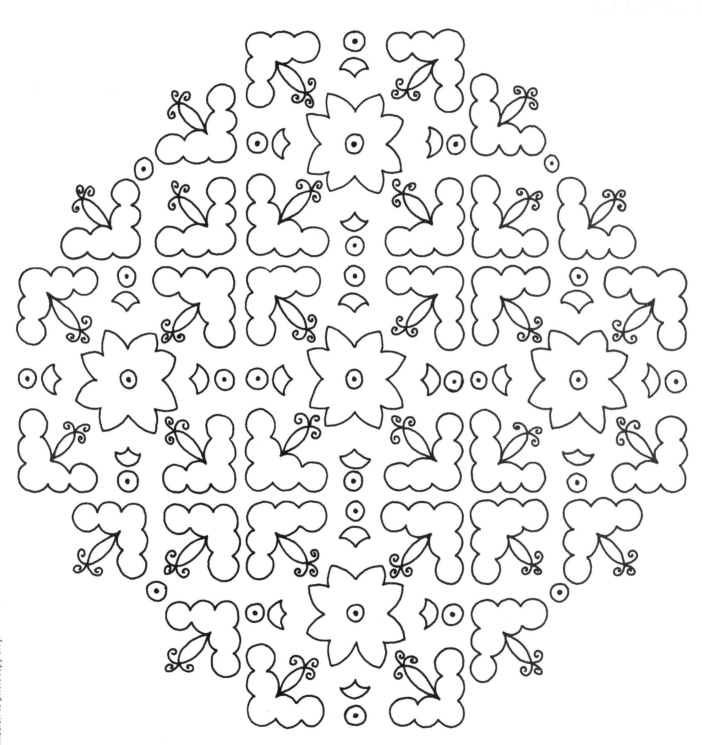

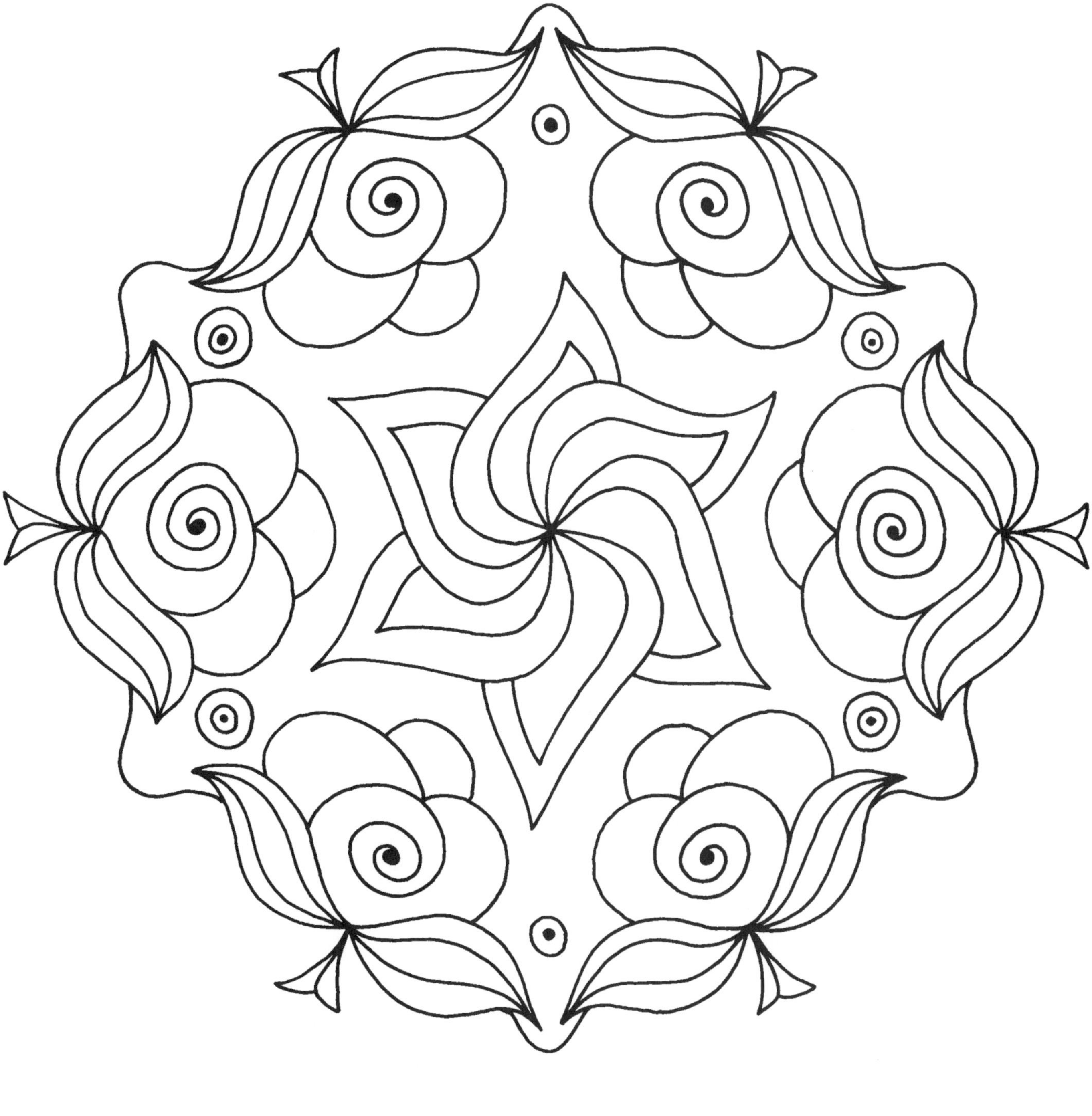

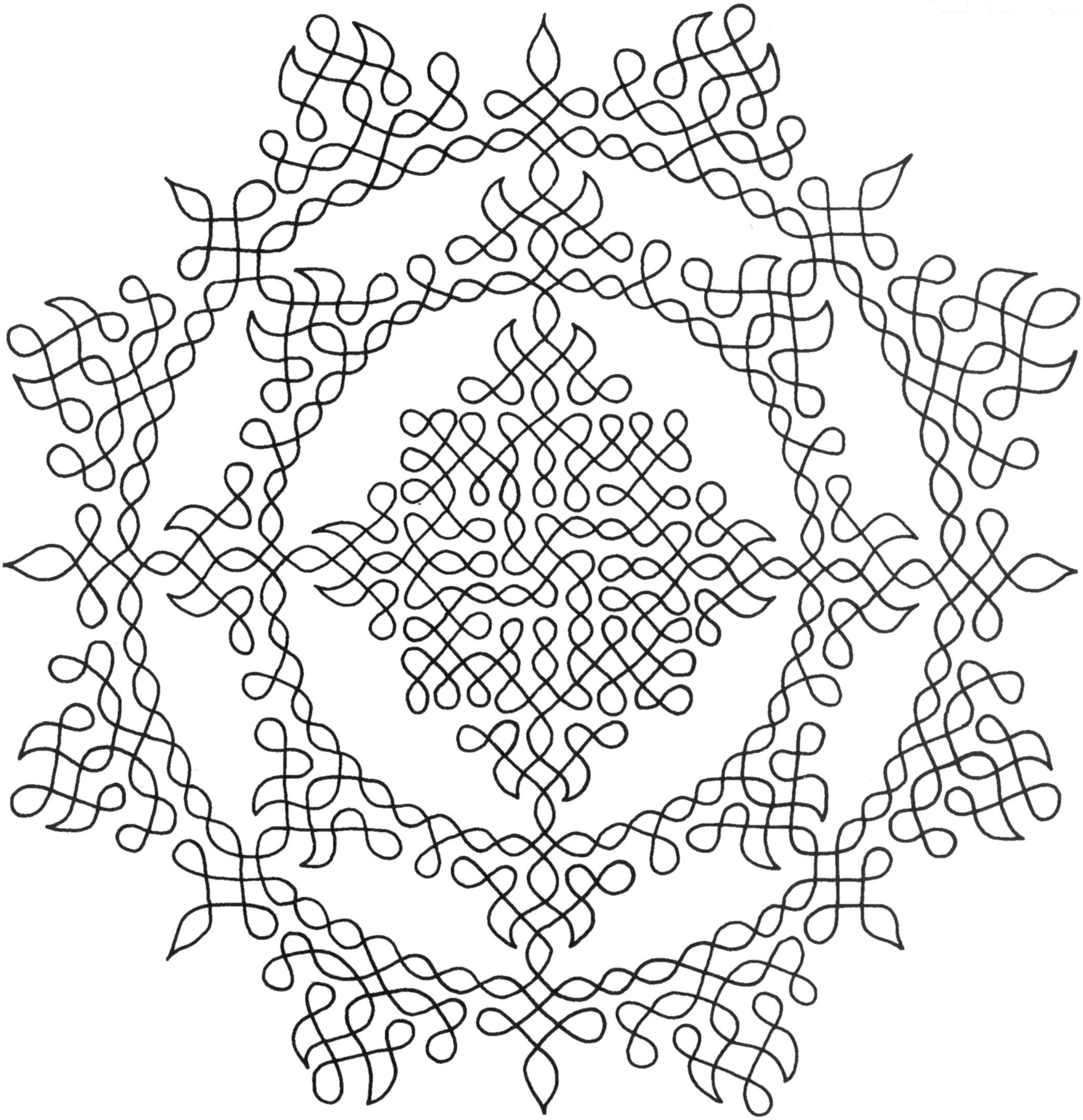

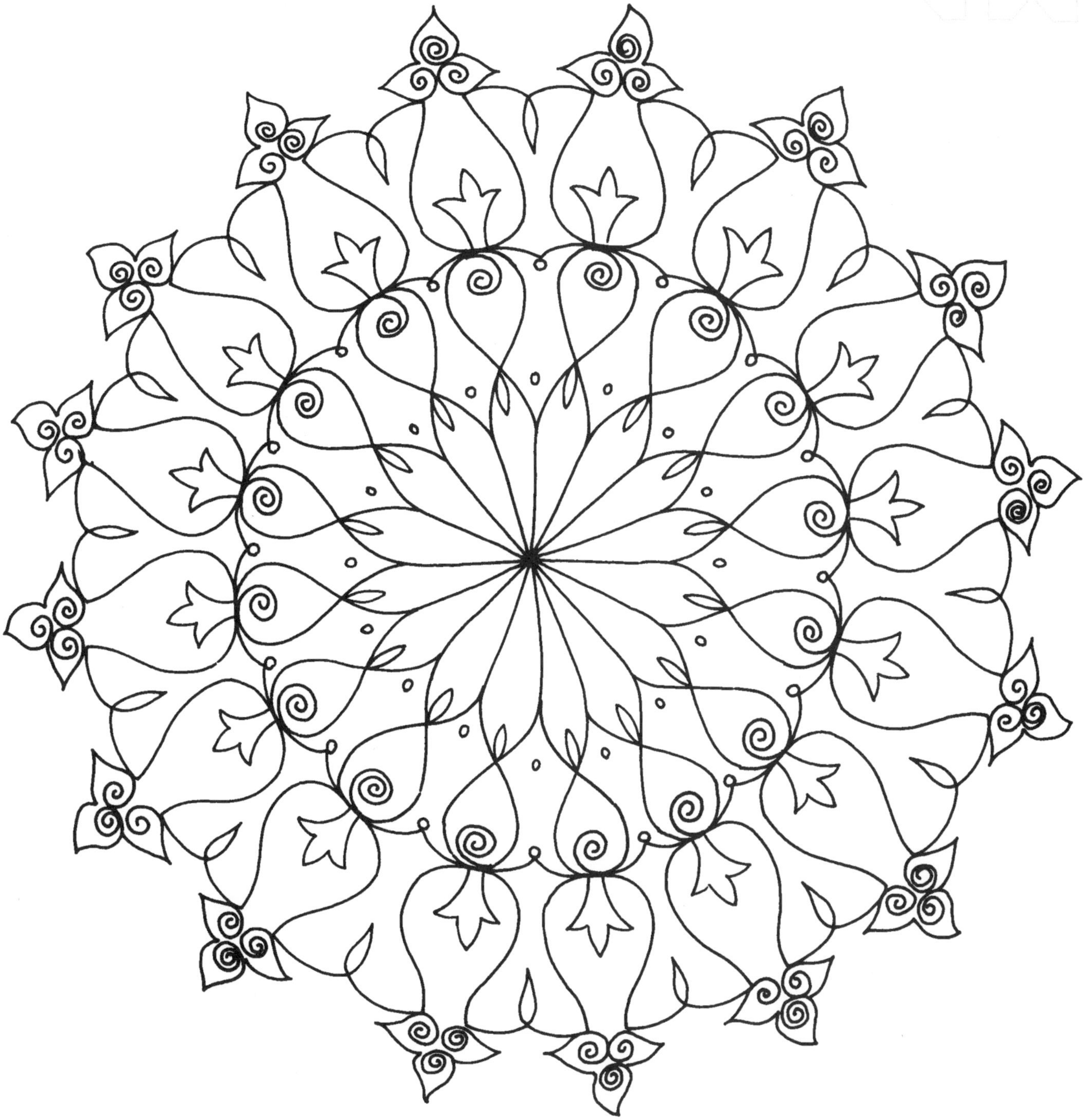

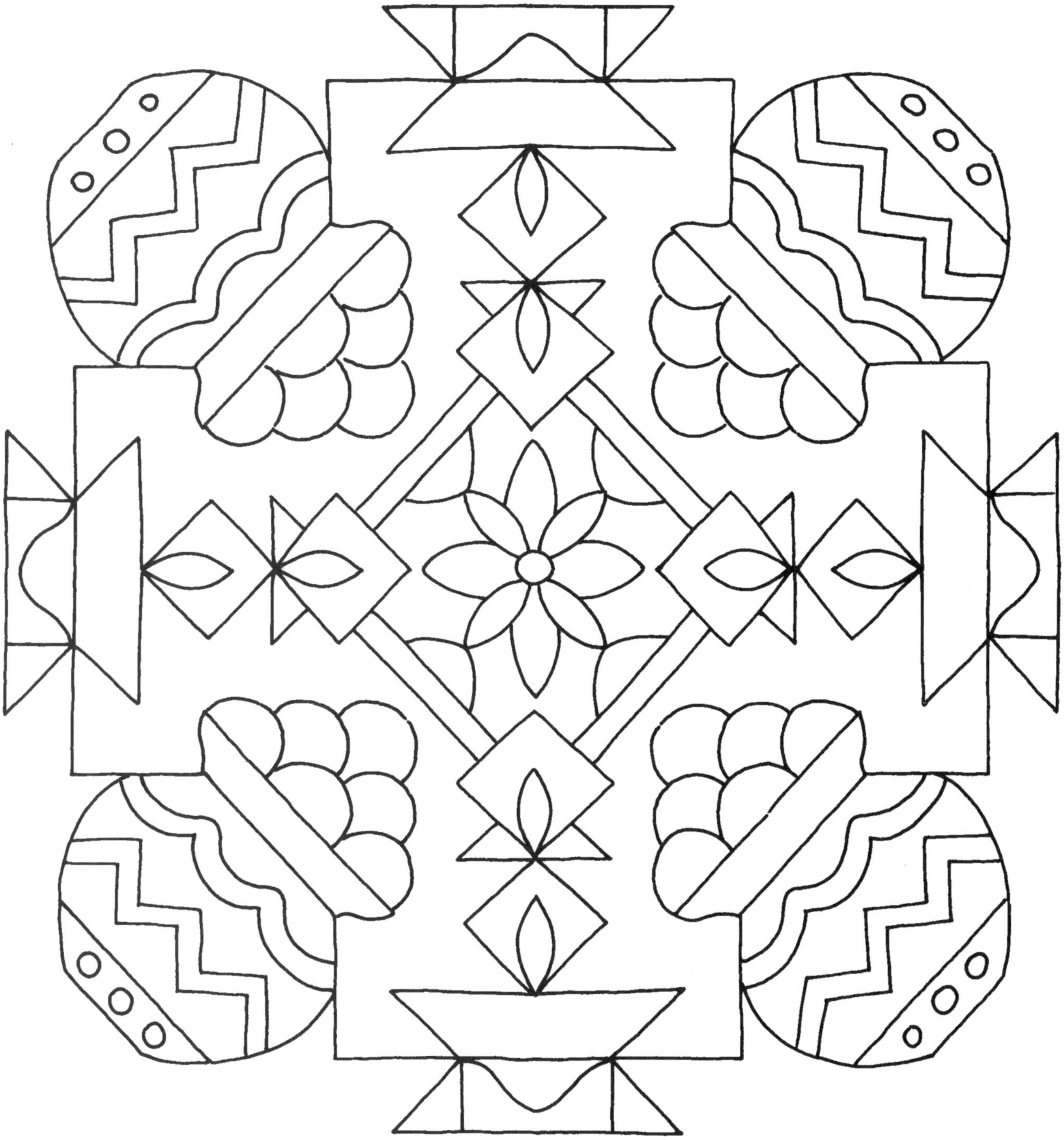

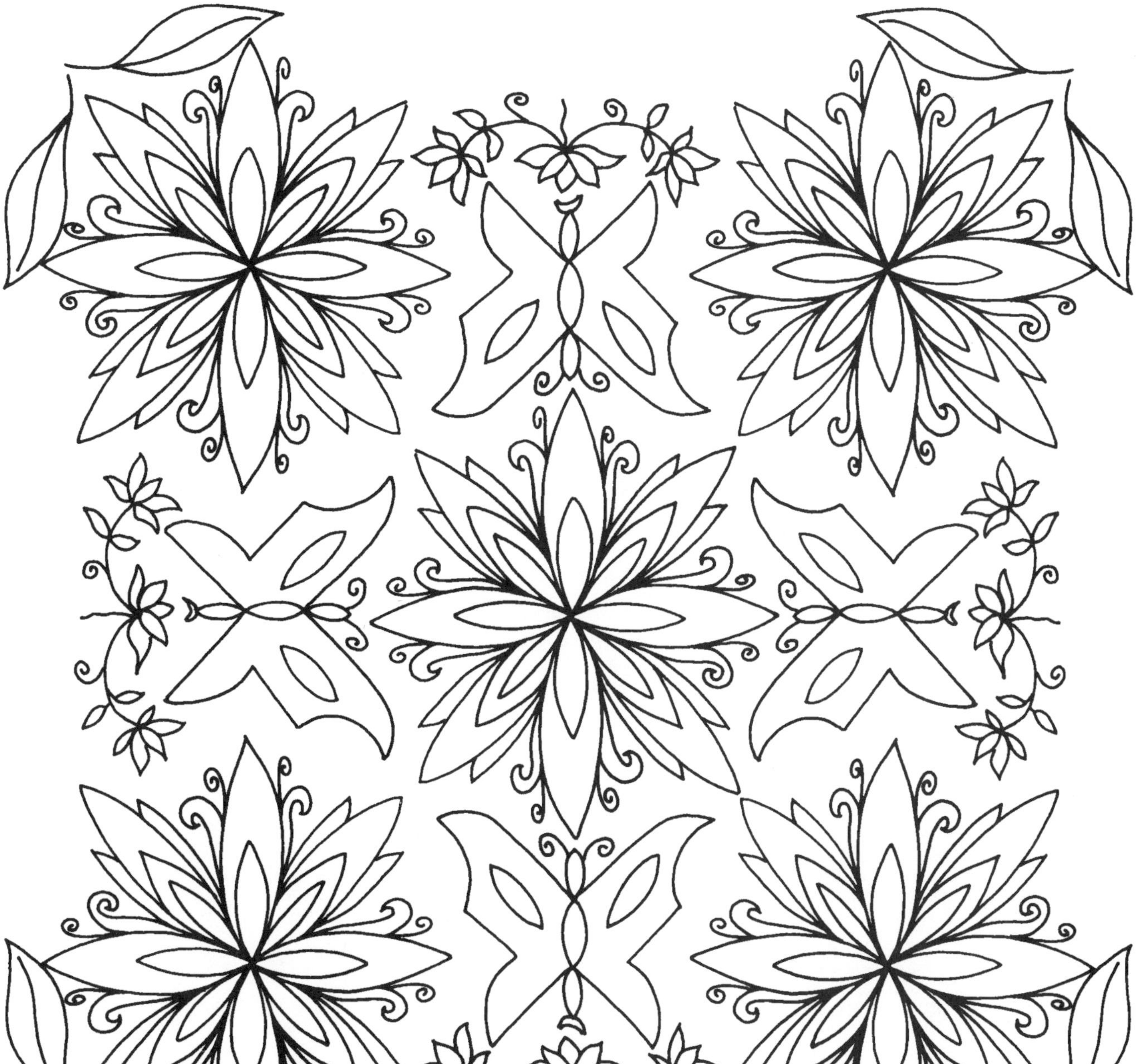

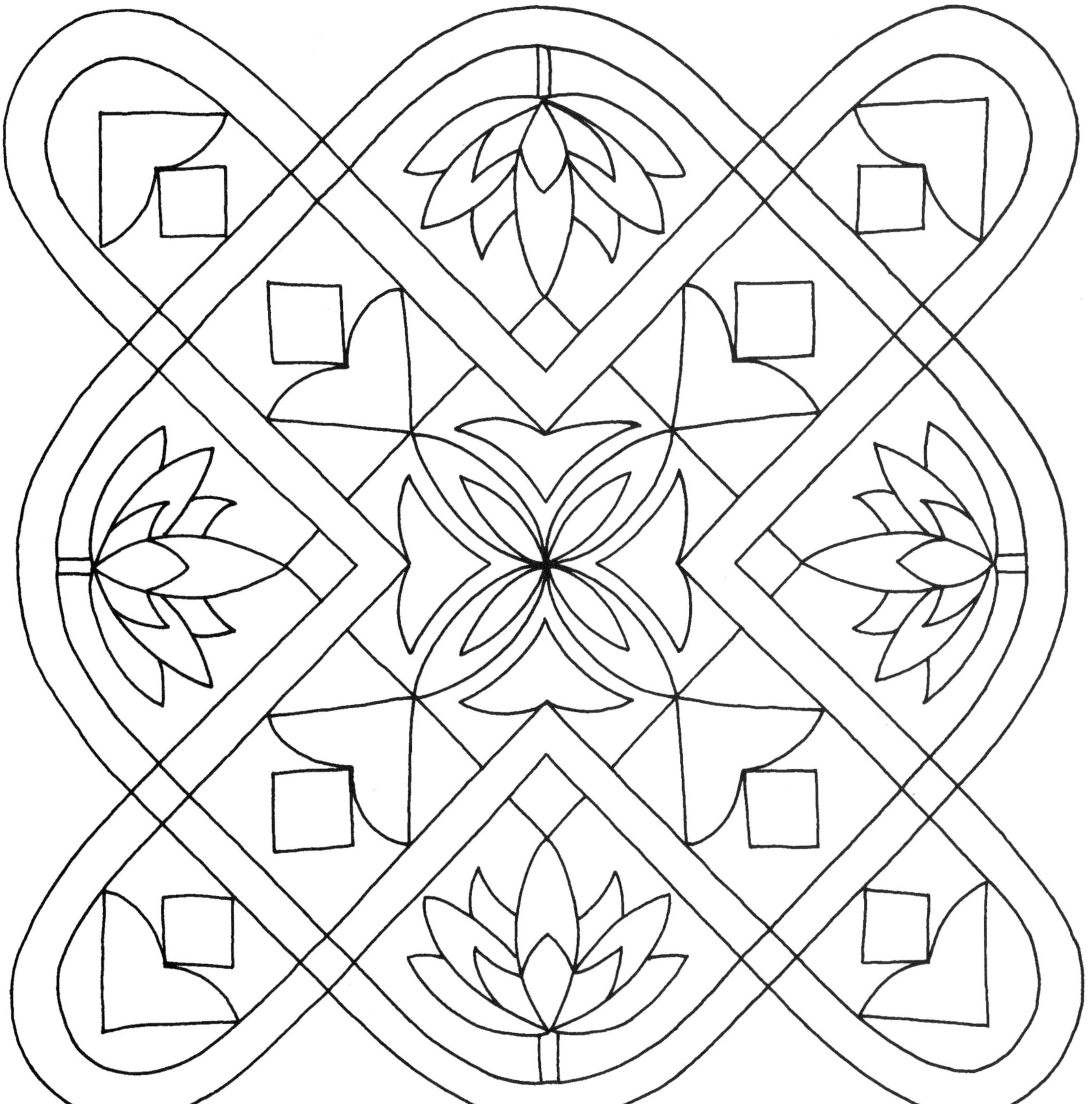

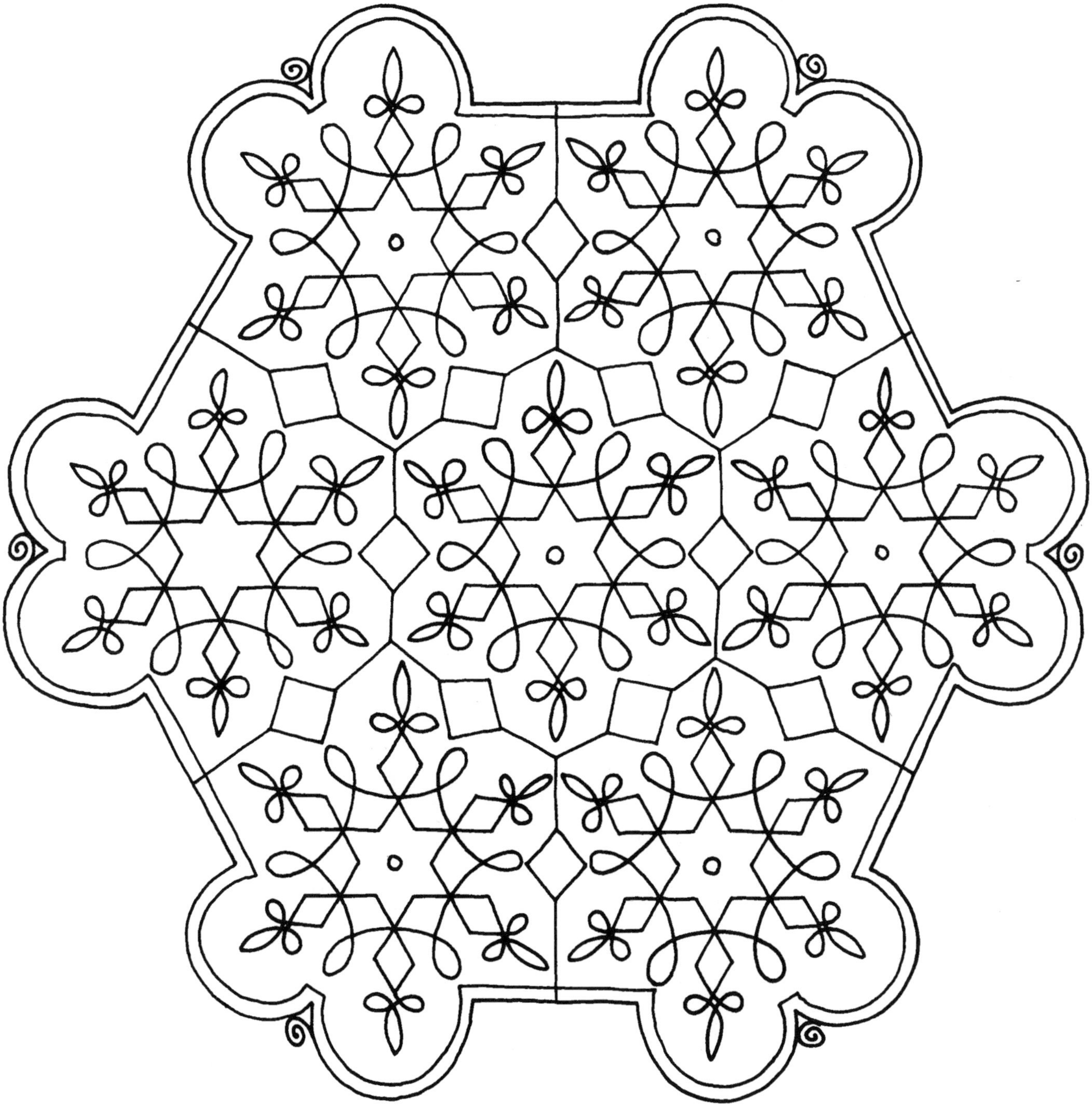

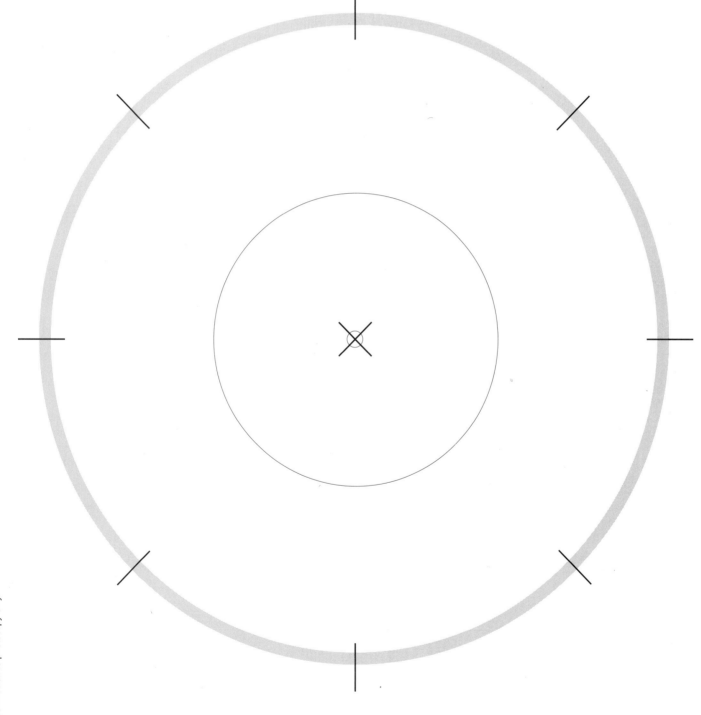

Magical Mandala Coloring Books from Hunter House

42 MANDALA PATTERNS COLORING BOOK

Wolfgang Hund

The mandalas in this book are drawn from the entire world of design and nature, mixing traditional designs with modern themes that appeal to children and adults. Nature elements such as trees, moons and stars reflect the environment, while animals such as fish, doves and butterflies remind us we are all part of universal life. Motifs repeat within mandalas in a soothing way that encourages us to revisit the images, finding new shapes and meanings in them. A perfect introduction to the joy of coloring mandalas.

96 pages ... 42 illus. ... Paperback $9.95

42 INDIAN MANDALAS COLORING BOOK

Monika Helwig

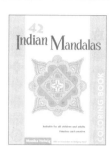

The mandalas in this book are based on ornamental patterns created in households and villages in India. Traditionally made of colored rice powder, flowers, leaves or colored sand, mandalas such as the ones in this book have been used to decorate homes, temples and meeting places. They may be used daily as well as on special occasions, and can be found in the homes of people of all faiths. The artists make each pattern different and special, using all their ingenuity and skill to increase the delight of all who see them.

96 pages ... 42 illus. ... Paperback $9.95

42 SEASONAL MANDALAS COLORING BOOK

Wolfgang Hund

The mandalas in this book are a mixture of Eastern and Western themes that will appeal to both the sophisticated and the primal in all of us. Luscious fruit, delicate flowers and detailed leaves and snowflakes are among the designs representing summer, spring, fall and winter, while more whimsical patterns include bunnies and spring chicks. You will also find jack-o-lanterns, Christmas scenes and New Year's noisemakers. Children can learn about the seasons and celebrate familiar holidays with these playful, intricate designs!

96 pages ... 42 illus. ... Paperback $9.95

SmartFun Activity Books from Hunter House

These activity books encourage creativity, concentration, and social activity in children. Appropriate age levels, times of play, and group sizes are indicated for every game. Most games are noncompetitive and none require special skills or training. The series is widely used in homes, schools, day-care centers, and summer camps.

101 MORE MUSIC GAMES FOR CHILDREN: New Fun and Learning with Rhythm and Song

by Jerry Storms

This book offers a wide array of song and dance activities from a variety of cultures. Besides listening, concentration, and expression games, it includes rhythm games, dance and movement games, relaxation games, and musical projects.

192 pp. ... 30 illus. ... Paperback $12.95 ... Spiral bound $17.95

101 DANCE GAMES FOR CHILDREN: Fun and Creativity with Movement

by Paul Rooyackers

This book encourages children to interact and express how they feel in creative fantasies and without words in meeting and greeting games, cooperation games, story dances, party dances, and more. No dance training or athletic skills are required.

160 pp. ... 30 illus. ... Paperback $12.95 ... Spiral bound $17.95

101 MUSIC GAMES FOR CHILDREN: Fun and Learning with Rhythm and Song

by Jerry Storms

This imaginative book is used to introduce children to learning about music and sound. Using audiocassettes or CDs, children and adults get to play listening games, concentration games, musical quizzes, and more.

160 pp. ... 30 illus. ... Paperback $12.95 ... Spiral bound $17.95

101 DRAMA GAMES FOR CHILDREN: Fun and Learning with Acting and Make-Believe

by Paul Rooyackers

Drama games are a dynamic form in which children explore their minds and the world and use their playacting in sensory games, pantomimes, story games with puppets, masks and costumes, and more.

160 pp. ... 30 illus. ... Paperback $12.95 ... Spiral bound $17.95